D1187210

THE TALE OF THE GOLDEN COCKEREL

ISBN 0 460 06777 X

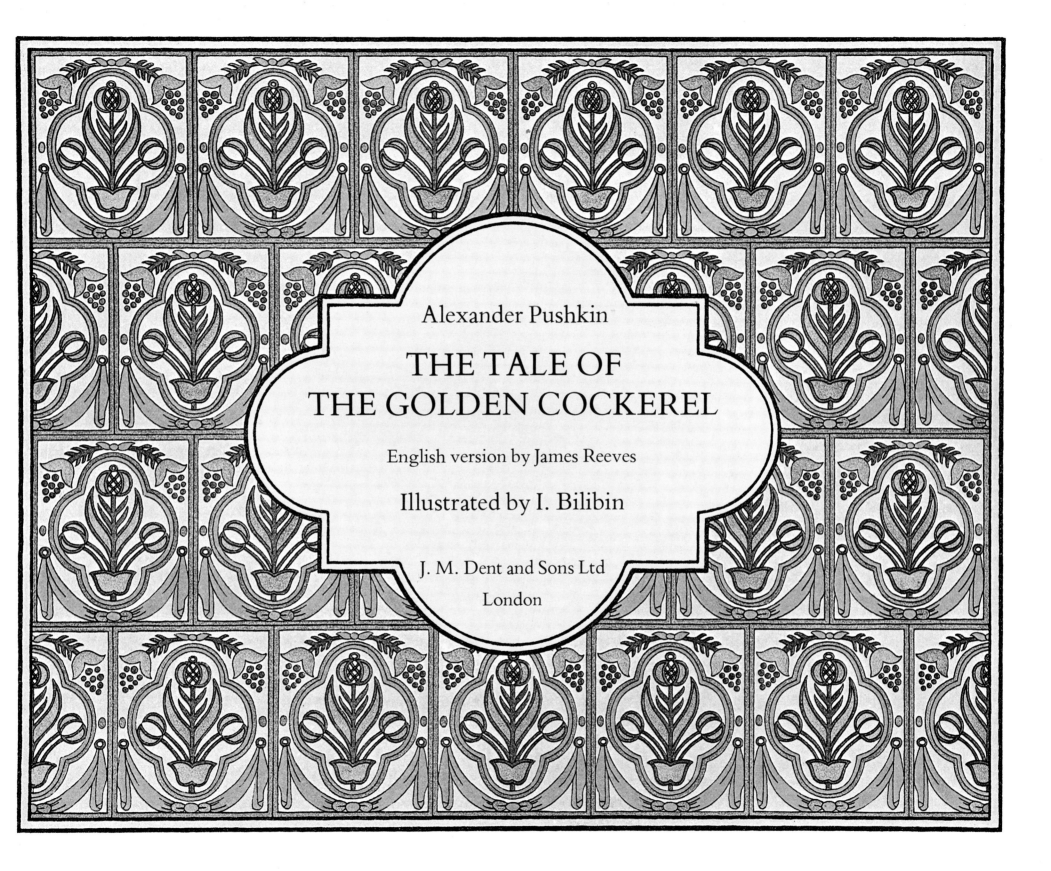

Alexander Pushkin

THE TALE OF
THE GOLDEN COCKEREL

English version by James Reeves

Illustrated by I. Bilibin

J. M. Dent and Sons Ltd

London

In a distant kingdom, farther than far, reigned good King Dodon. In youth he had been warlike, never leaving the nearby countries in peace. Time passed. The King grew old. His thoughts turned to peace. To enjoy a life of ease and quiet—that was all he wished for now. But the men of nearby lands wanted revenge. They raided King Dodon's borders, leaving death and destruction behind them. Dodon was forced to keep a large army to do battle all along his frontiers. His soldiers were keen and watchful, but they were never in time to stop the raiders. When Dodon's soldiers marched south, the raiders would turn up in the east. When the soldiers set forth to fight them, they would appear from the sea.

So poor King Dodon wept tears of rage and could not sleep at night.

"I will speak to a wise man," he said, "a magician who understands the stars."

So a rider was sent forth to fetch the magician to the palace. The magician came carrying a bag, and out of the bag he took a golden cockerel.

"O King," he said, "take this bird and set him up on a high steeple. He will be your sentinel. When things are quiet he will sit still. But when there is war or rumour of war he will lift up his red comb, ruffle his bright plumes, crow with all his might and turn towards the threatened danger."

The King was delighted. He thanked the wise man and said:

"For such service no reward is too great. Ask me what you will. Your very first wish shall be granted, even as if it were my own."

So, sitting high up on a steeple, the little cockerel became guardian of Dodon's kingdom. As soon as there was trouble on the borders he would ruffle his feathers, turn towards the danger and sing out:

"Hear my cock-a-doodle shrill!
Sleep in peace and fear no ill."

Then the people on Dodon's borders stopped raiding his kingdom and settled down in peace.

So a year passed and then another. All

was peace, and the cockerel was silent on his high perch.

Then one day King Dodon was roused from his slumber by a terrible noise outside his window.

"Wake up, O King and Father of our people!" cried the captain of the guard. "There is bad news."

Dodon sat up and yawned.

"What's all the fuss?" he cried. "What is this dreadful news?"

"The cockerel is crowing fit to burst!" said the captain. "The city is in panic."

The King looked out of the window. There, sure enough, high on his perch the cockerel was turning to the east, his comb upright, his feathers ruffled.

There was no time to lose. Dodon sent an army eastward under the command of his elder son. At once the cockerel was still. The noise in the city died down. The King went back to bed.

A whole week passed, and no news came from his army. Dodon did not even know if there had been a battle. Then once more the cockerel crowed.

Immediately a second army was sent eastward under the command of the King's younger son, to bring help to his older brother. Again the cockerel was quiet, and again no rider came to the city bringing news.

When another week had passed the same panic seized the people, as once more the cockerel sounded the alarm.

This time the old King decided to lead an army himself, though he was not sure it was wise for him to go.

With Dodon at their head the soldiers marched day and night, mile after mile.

They were almost dead with weariness when, on the eighth day, they came to a range of mountains. On the march to the mountains they were surprised to see neither battlefield nor burial ground. But what they saw at last, in one of the valleys between the mountains, surprised them still more.

A beautiful silken tent fluttered in the breeze, and around it lay the bodies of the King's soldiers, slain in battle. There was utter silence. Dodon hurried to the tent, and there, outside its entrance, he saw the dead bodies of his two sons. Neither had helmet or armour, but each held a sword, thrust into the other's heart. Heads bent, the riderless horses strayed over the blood-soaked grass.

In grief and anguish the King cried out:

"Alas, my sons, and woe betide us all. Who has trapped in his cunning nets our brave falcons?"

And the voices of Dodon's soldiers echoed his words along the desolate valley.

Then the curtains that veiled the entrance to the silken tent were drawn aside. There appeared before the King's eyes the lovely Queen of Shemakhan. Dodon fell silent. As he gazed into the eyes of the Queen, the death of his two sons was forgotten. The Queen smiled at Dodon, curtsied low and took him by the hand. She led him inside her tent. She made him sit at her table and eat of the choicest foods. When he had finished she let him rest upon her brocaded couch.

For a whole week King Dodon obeyed the Queen's wishes like a slave and passed his time pleasantly in her silken tent.

Then he began to think of returning to his city. His soldiers wanted to go back to their wives. So, taking the fair Queen by the hand, Dodon set out on the journey home.

The news of Dodon's return had gone before him. As he approached the city the crowds came out to welcome him and his young Queen. Dodon graciously thanked the people for their welcome. Then, amidst the crowd, he beheld his old counsellor, the magician.

И. БИЛИБИНЪ. 1906.

He looked shabby but still wore his magician's hat.

"Greetings to you, wise old man," cried Dodon. "Come closer and tell me how things go with you."

"Greetings, O King," said the magician. "Now is the time for our reckoning. Do you recall how, when I served you in the hour of your need, you promised me anything I might wish? Give me as my reward the beauteous Queen of Shemakhan."

King Dodon was dumbfounded.

"Are you mad?" he demanded. "The devil take you for a madman! True, I promised you all you wished, but you can wish too much. Do you not know who I am? You shall have gold and silver. You shall have a high-sounding title. You shall have the finest horse in my stable or half my kingdom. Any of these things I will give you gladly."

"I want nothing," answered the magician, "but the Queen of Shemakhan."

In a rage Dodon spat on the ground.

"You are too bold, wretched old man," he cried. "You will get nothing—nothing, I say! You had better go while your body is still whole. Take the old fool out of my sight!"

The magician opened his mouth in

protest. But Dodon, infuriated, raised his sceptre and struck him on the head. The magician fell dead at the King's feet.

Horror came over the city, and a shudder ran through the crowd. In the terrible silence that followed the shrill laughter of the Queen rang out for all to hear. The King was deeply troubled, but smiled lovingly upon the Queen and told his coachman to drive on. As the royal coach entered the palace gates a rustling sound was heard from above. The golden cockerel flew down from his perch on the steeple and alighted on the carriage. Then he pecked viciously at the King's head. Dodon toppled from the coach and fell dead on the roadside. The bird flew off into farthest space.

As for the Queen of Shemakhan, she vanished into air and disappeared as if she had never been.

Some say that the ghostly voice of the cockerel was heard to call:

"This story, be it false or true,
Something, young men, it may
teach you."